Emma Dodd

PRESENTS

CINDERELEPHANT

templar publishing

Once upon a time there was
a lonely girl called Cinderelephant.

Cinderelephant lived with her two cousins, who were known as
The Warty Sisters. They were horrible, mean and smelly
and they had no table manners.

They made Cinderelephant do all the cooking and cleaning
and they **never**, ever said, "Thank you."

Cinderelephant was sad and tired and fed up
with being ignored.

One day, an invitation arrived from the palace. Prince Trunky had decided it was time he found a girlfriend, so King Saggy and Queen Wrinkly had invited **all** the girls in the neighbourhood to a ball.

Invitation

The Warty Sisters were very excited and started to plan what they would wear.

"If they are inviting all the girls," said Cinderelephant, "perhaps that includes me!"

"Of course you won't be going, Cinder-irrelevant!" laughed the Warty Sisters. "Whoever would want to dance with **you**?"

The day of the party arrived and the Warty Sisters
dressed up in their most fashionable clothes.

"Bye-bye, Cinderelephant!" they called as they left the house.
"Don't wait up – we're bound to be home very late!"

Poor Cinderelephant sat all
alone in the silent house.

A **big** tear rolled down her trunk
and plopped onto the floor.

"Hey," squeaked a small voice.
"Watch where you drop those tears! I'm getting soaked!"

Cinderelephant saw a tiny mouse looking up at her crossly.
"I'm sorry," she sniffed, "I'm just feeling sad that I can't go
to the party. Excuse me for asking, but **who** are you?"

"Why, I'm your **Furry Godmouse**, of course!" he exclaimed.
And with a flick of his magical tail he said...

"You shall go to the ball!"

"Wow, you look amazing! Go to the party and enjoy yourself," said the Furry Godmouse, "but,

and it's a big but...

you **must** be home by midnight."

At the palace,
Prince Trunky was bored.
He didn't want to dance
with any of the girls – he was
worried they might get
squashed! If only he
could find someone a bit
more his type...

But wait!
Who was this vision of loveliness
that had just walked in?

"Clear the floor!" bellowed Prince Trunky.

"Wanna dance?"
he asked Cinderelephant, as he swept her
off her feet and onto the dance floor.

Prince Trunky
and Cinderelephant danced
together for the rest of
the evening.

"Who is that?"
everybody asked enviously.
"She looks a bit like... but no,
it can't be – she looks so good
and she's such a great mover!"
said the Warty Sisters.

Cinderelephant
had never been so happy.
She didn't notice the
time passing until
suddenly the clock
struck midnight.
"Oops!" she exclaimed,
"I've got to go home!"

As she rushed from the palace,
she dropped one of her
beautiful shoes.

"Wait! What's your name?" Prince Trunky called after her, but Cinderelephant had already gone.

At his feet lay one of Cinderelephant's fabulous shoes.

Then and there, Prince Trunky made a decision
(and Prince Trunky's decisions carry a lot of weight).

Picking up the stiletto, he declared, "I shall find the girl
whose foot fits this shoe – and I shall **marry** her!"

The next day Prince Trunky began the search
for the girl of his dreams.

He went from house to house trying the
fabulous shoe on every girl's foot.

It fitted nobody.

"Will I **never** find her?" sighed the prince.

At last he arrived at the
Warty Sisters' house.

"Give me that shoe," demanded one Warty Sister. "It's bound to fit me!"
But of course her little trotter was
far too small for the gorgeous shoe.

"Let me have a go," said the other sister, snatching it.
"I am Prince Trunky's one true love!"
But of course it did not fit her either.

Sighing quietly to herself, Cinderelephant peeped shyly
through a crack in the kitchen door.

But... **whoops!**
She accidentally stepped into a bucket,
knocking over the mop, bringing a pile of pots and pans
crashing and clattering down.

"Who is in there?"
asked the prince.
"Oh, nobody important!"
said the Warty Sisters hurriedly.
Taking no notice, Prince Trunky
went to investigate.

"Could it be you?" asked the prince,
slipping the lovely shoe onto
Cinderelephant's foot.
It was a perfect fit.

"You are the one for me!"
cried the prince in delight.

Cinderelephant had never been so
enormously excited in her life.

Cinderelephant and Prince Trunky were married the very next day.

And, of course, they were **hugely** happy ever after.

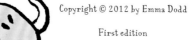

For Rose and Fay, with love from Emma xx

A TEMPLAR BOOK

First published in the UK in 2012 by Templar Publishing,
an imprint of The Templar Company Limited,
The Granary, North Street, Dorking, Surrey, RH4 1DN, UK
www.templarco.co.uk

ISBN 978-1-84877-782-8

Written by Emma Dodd
Edited by Jenny Broom

Printed in China